Book 4

PARTY ON PLUTO

BY JEFF DINARDO
ILLUSTRATED BY DAVE CLEGG

RED
CHAIR
•PRESS•

Funny Bone Books

and Funny Bone Readers are produced and published by
Red Chair Press LLC   PO Box 333   South Egremont, MA 01258-0333
www.redchairpress.com

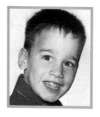

About the Author

Jeff Dinardo's books are filled with humor and silliness that captures a child's imagination. When not writing, Jeff runs a successful design firm specializing in textbooks for use in classrooms from K-8.

About the Artist

Dave Clegg lives and works on a small horse farm in north Georgia with his wife Lyn. All of Dave's work is done digitally on his computer. When he is not drawing, he can be found creating songs with his guitar or making robot sculptures!

PPublisher's Cataloging-In-Publication Data
Names: Dinardo, Jeffrey. | Clegg, Dave, illustrator.
Title: The Jupiter twins. Book 4, Party on Pluto / by Jeff Dinardo ; illustrated by Dave Clegg.
Other Titles: Party on Pluto

Description: South Egremont, MA : Red Chair Press, [2018] | Series: Funny bone books. First
    chapters | Interest age level: 005-007. | Summary: "Trudy and Tina are best friends. They
    are also twins. Trudy loves adventure and Tina is happy to go along for the ride--as long
    as it is a smooth ride! Who doesn't enjoy a party? And this party is their favorite teacher's
    wedding. First Chapters books are easy introductions to exploring longer text."--Provided by
    publisher.

Identifiers: LCCN 2017934022 | ISBN 978-1-63440-252-1 (library hardcover)
    | ISBN 978-1-63440-256-9 (paperback) | ISBN 978-1-63440-260-6 (ebook)

Subjects: LCSH: Twins--Juvenile fiction. | Pluto (Planet)--Juvenile fiction. | Outer space--
    Exploration--Juvenile fiction. | Parties--Juvenile fiction. | CYAC: Twins--Fiction. | Pluto
    (Planet)--Fiction. | Outer space--Exploration--Fiction. | Parties--Fiction.

Classification: LCC PZ7.D6115 Jup 2018 (print) | LCC PZ7.D6115 (ebook) | DDC [E]--dc23

Printed in Canada

102017 1P FRNS18

CONTENTS

Meet the Characters

Trudy

Tina

Ms. Bickleblorb

Max

A Long Ride

The roar of the rocket engines quieted to a hum as the ship gently touched down on Pluto.

It had been a long ride from Jupiter. Tina had slept most of the way, but her twin sister Trudy kept busy. She had just finished reading her newest mystery novel, *The Strange Disappearance on Neptune's Moons.*

"Wake up," said Trudy as she closed her book. "We're finally here."

Tina yawned and rubbed her eyes as the twins grabbed their bags and hopped off the ship.

Their teacher, Ms. Bickleblorb was waiting for them.

"Oh girls, you made it!" she said as she gave them each a hug. "I couldn't imagine getting married without you both here."

"Why are you getting married all the way on Pluto?" asked Tina before a yawn.

"It's Max's idea," she said. "Isn't he so romantic? He wants to get married on New Year's Day and that's a special day here."

"Why is that?" asked Tina.

"I know," said Trudy. "Because Pluto only has a New Year's Day once every 247 years!"

"Wow," said Tina.

2 MAX

When the ceremony was about to start, everyone was in their place except Max, the man Ms. Bickleblorb was going to marry.

"Where is he?" Ms. Bickleblorb asked.

"I smell trouble," said Trudy. "Let's find him."

Tina and Trudy slipped outside and
found Max sitting on the steps crying.

"I can't believe it," he said as he
slapped his head with his hand. "How
can I be so forgetful?"

"What's wrong?" said Trudy.

Max looked up and saw the twins.

"The rings!" he said. "I lost the rings!"
Trudy nodded and took out her
notebook.

"I love a good mystery," she said.
"Where was the last place you had them?"

Max thought for a second.

"I know I had them this morning when
I got dressed," he said. "But when I got
here they were gone."

"Where did you go today?" Trudy asked.

"First I went to see the baker to check on the wedding cake," said Max.

Trudy wrote that down.

"Then I met with the band to go over the wedding songs," said Max.

Trudy wrote that down.

"Lastly, I stopped to see the florist to check on the flowers," said Max.

Trudy wrote that down too.

"Don't worry Max," said Trudy. "We'll solve this mystery."

"We will?" mumbled Tina.

3 THE BAKER

Trudy and Tina stood outside a shop with a sign overhead that read "Renée's Best Bakery."

Trudy looked at the list in her notebook. "This is the place," she said. "Let's go."

A tall alien smiled as they came in. The twins guessed she was Renée.

"Can I help you?" the alien said. "Would you like a Plutonian blue velvet cupcake?"

Tina looked at the delicious dessert and realized she was hungry. "I'll take two of the cupcakes to go please," she said.

"That's not why we are here," Trudy scolded. "Our friend Max lost his wedding rings and we wanted to see if he left them here."

"Oh my," said Renée. "I don't think so, but let's look."

The three of them searched the whole
bakery, but there were no rings.

The twins thanked Renée anyway.

Trudy looked at her notebook.
"Let's go see the band," she said as
she started to walk out the door.

"Wait!" said Renée. She handed them
a box with two cupcakes in it.

"Good luck!"

🚀 THE BAND

Down the street was the second shop.
Its sign read "Frankie's Music Emporium."

They were just about to enter when the
door flew open and a short, three-headed,
six-armed alien came running out. It
almost knocked the girls over.

One set of arms held a violin, another held a flute, and the third pair of hands held an instrument the girls had never seen before.

"We are here to see the band about Max's wedding," Trudy said quickly.

"Yes, yes, that's us," the first head said.

"And we are already late," said the second head.

"We should have left an hour ago," said the third head.

Before the twins could ask anything else the alien was gone.

Trudy looked up at the sign again.

"I wonder which one was Frankie?" she said.

5 THE FLORIST

"Let's hope we have better luck with the florist," said Trudy as they stood outside the next shop. Its sign above simply said "Flowers."

Tina and Trudy opened the door. They saw the owner chatting with a customer as he wrapped up a very large bunch of unusual flowers.

"These will look amazing on the table," he said.

"We have to talk to him quickly," said Tina.

Trudy wasn't paying attention to her sister. She was staring at a very large potted plant that stood right behind the customer.

As the customer chatted with the
owner, Trudy saw the green plant reach
into the man's pocket and pull out a
watch. The plant quickly slipped it into
its own planter then stood still again.

"*Jumping Jupiter,*" Trudy whispered
to her sister. "I think I know what
happened to the rings."

The shop owner finished wrapping the flowers and helped the customer carry them out.

When they were gone Trudy walked up to the plant.

"Our friend Max was in today," she said to the plant. "And I think you stole the rings he had in his pocket."

The plant wiggled a bit. "Could be," it snarled.

Tina blinked.

"You can talk?" she said.

"What's it to you?" said the plant.

"Why don't you kids run along now."

Trudy knew she had her thief.

"I'm not leaving until you give me those rings back!" she said as she scowled at the plant. The plant seemed to scowl back at her.

Tina rushed between them. "Will you trade for them?" she asked.

The plant seemed to consider this. "What have you got to trade?" it said.

"Yeah," said Trudy. "What have we got to trade?"

Tina reached into her pack and took out a box. "How about two delicious Plutonian cupcakes?" she said.

The plant shivered with delight. "Are they blue velvet?" it asked.

"Of course!" said Tina.

Before they could say another word,
the plant reached deep into its base
and pulled out the two rings. It plopped
them in Tina's hand. Then it grabbed
the cupcakes.

"Good trade," the plant said.

Trudy and Tina smiled and ran from
the store.

Max was still crying on the steps, but now Ms. Bickleblorb was next to him.

"I don't care about the rings," she said. "I just want you."

"Well now you can have both," said
Trudy.

Tina opened her hand and gave the
rings to Max.

"Come on, we have a wedding to go to."

As the sun rose on a New Year on Pluto, Ms. Bickleblorb and Max were married.

All the guests applauded as loudly as they could, especially the Jupiter twins.

"I hope they serve Plutonian cupcakes," said Tina. "I'm starving!"